DART THE DIGITAL REINDEER

Santa's Partner in the Cyber World

by Byron Butterworth

Illustrated by Madeleine Mae Migallos

For my remarkable Grandchildren
Max, Sylvie, Vivian, Peregrine, and Filigree

Other pieces by Dr. Butterworth include
A book of short stories
SHADOWY PLACES

Short films on YouTube and Prime Video
The Stolen Word
Dappled Gardens 1
Dappled Gardens 2
Dappled Gardens 3
A Forest of Secret Treasures

Dr. Butterworth lives in North Carolina with his wife.
Amy Johnson, and their Welsh Terrier, Lilly

Dart the Digital Reindeer
Copyright © 2021 by Byron Butterworth

Tellwell Talent
www.tellwell.ca

ISBN
978-0-2288-5489-0 (Hardcover)
978-0-2288-5490-6 (Paperback)

The amazing story of Dart the Digital Reindeer

Sylvie got her first computer as a Christmas present when she was just nine years old. Over the years, she got better and better at programming lifelike characters that would dance on the screen. To her friends, it appeared that creating the moving pictures was as easy for Sylvie as rubbing a puppy's tummy.

Ms. Lafferty, the advisor to the high school Computer Graphics Club, had seen some of Sylvie's work and had invited her to meet with the Club, even though Sylvie was still just in middle school. Sylvie already knew a few of the Club members from sharing animations with them online, and was thrilled to attend her first meeting. Sylvie sat up straight and listened to Ms. Lafferty.

"Good afternoon, students," Ms. Lafferty said. "I have some exciting news. We just got a license for the amazing new CyberMax 2001 animation program. You can either work with it

here or on your home computer. Your assignment is to create an original character and make it come to life on the screen. I'll work with each of you individually. Now, let's see what you can create."

Sylvie couldn't wait to tell her parents — and get started on the assignment. She rushed home after the club meeting and waited for them. As soon as they got home from work, she herded her mom and dad into the family room.

Sylvie gestured with her hands as she described the powerful new computer program and the project assignment. Her parents exchanged knowing glances, pleased with their daughter's enthusiasm.

"The thing is," Sylvie continued, "we'll have to get a new computer to accommodate the program so that I can work at home. Can we do that?"

Her dad said, "Well, let your mom and I talk it over."

"OK," Sylvie said and plopped on a couch at the far end of the room. Her dog, a Welsh Terrier named Lilly, jumped up and sat next to her.

Her folks spoke quietly as Christmas lights began to twinkle on in the neighborhood.

After a few minutes, that seemed like forever, they walked over to Sylvie. "Sweetie," her dad began, "we'd love to support your project. But the computer would cost so much that it would have to be your only Christmas present. Would that be OK with you?"

"Yes, yes," she beamed, jumping up from the couch and hugging her mom with such force that she nearly pushed her over.

A few days later, the school's IT team finished installing the CyberMax 2001 program on Sylvie's new work station in her bedroom. The whole family, including Lilly, stood admiring the large, high-definition computer monitor displaying the words: "WELCOME."

"There you go, hon," her dad said. "Merry early Christmas."
"You've got this, Sylvie!" her mom exclaimed, gathering her up in a hug. "I can't wait to see what you'll do."

Once her parents were gone, Sylvie sat on her bed to collect her thoughts. Her dog jumped up and sat next to her. "Well, Lilly, what character should I create?"

Lilly tilted her head, as though she understood.

Sylvie sat for some time with her chin in her hands. The only sound was a soft bubbling from her aquarium in the corner.

Finally, she looked up, smiled and said, "I know, I'll create a reindeer. A reindeer for Santa, but one that lives in the cyber world, rather than the North Pole!"

From then on, Sylvie spent every free moment on her task. She studied hundreds of pictures and videos of reindeer. What was the shape of their bodies? What was the color of their fur and what did the hair look like up close? How did they walk, run, and leap? Slowly, Sylvie's reindeer began to take shape.

Because her creation had to be good enough for Santa, she gave it a voice, as well. As she worked on the animation, she would talk to it. Her reindeer would talk back to her, but only with the phrases she had programmed it to say.

On the last day of school before Christmas vacation, Sylvie
showed Ms. Lafferty her virtual reindeer. Her teacher spent a long

time exploring how the animation reproduced the movements of the real animal and she admired how very lifelike it was.

Ms. Lafferty shook her head slowly. "Sylvie, your work is astonishing. This is as good as any animation I've seen."

"I really enjoyed making my reindeer more and more realistic." Sylvie said, excitedly. "This is the most fun I've ever had!"

By this point, the other students had left, and the classroom was quiet. "Well, my dear, if it were any better, it'd come to life." She took a deep breath and spoke slowly. "Sylvie, you have a gift.

That's a very rare and special thing. If you use your gift to be creative and to do good, it will be rewarding for you, and so many others, all of your life."

"OK," she nodded, eyes shining with pride.

Her teacher smiled, "Have a nice vacation. See you in the new year."

"Thanks so much," Sylvie beamed. She left the school and began walking home in the twilight. Little did she know what an enchanted evening was awaiting her.

After dinner, Sylvie went upstairs to put the final touches on her creation. "Well that's as perfect as I can make you," she whispered to the reindeer.

Just then her computer froze. The outside edges of the screen began to shimmer in a rapidly-changing rainbow of colors. She felt a breeze brush across her face, even though the windows were closed. Lilly jumped up and gave a warning bark and growled. Sylvie wondered if she'd been transported into some sort of a dream.

Then, the reindeer on the screen turned to her and asked, "Where am I?"

Astonished, Sylvie exclaimed, "Oh my gosh! Have you come to life? Are you talking to me?"

"Oh hello. Yes I'm alive, I can see and hear you," the reindeer said.

"What's your name?" he continued.

"I'm Sylvie."

"So, Sylvie, how did I get here?"

Sylvie swallowed hard, "Actually, I created you as a computer model, but something magical has happened, and now you've come to life."

The reindeer walked around inside the monitor for a few moments, pondering what Sylvie had told him. "I have a question. Why can't I touch you?" he asked.

"Well, I live in the physical world, and you live in cyber space.

We can see each other through this window but we can't go from one realm to the other."

    "But we can talk to each other and be friends, right?"

    "Yes, of course. I'd like that very much."

    "What's your world like?" Sylvie asked the reindeer.

    "Hmm, let me take a look around." The reindeer went away, leaving only his outline on the screen.

A couple of minutes later, he returned. "This cyber sphere is
a most amazing place. I can go to any part of the digital world in
an instant, from the New York Stock Exchange, to a cell phone in
China. I can see any program or email or electronic document."
"Did you meet anyone else like you?"

"Not really. The whole place is abuzz with activity, but it's all hardware and electronic bits and bytes. As far as I can see, I'm the only being in cyber space who can think for himself."

"Wow," Sylvie exclaimed. "That's incredible."

The reindeer turned to his creator, paused and then asked, "Sylvie, do I have a name?"

"Well, I've been thinking about that. Since you can move at the speed of light, I'm going to call you Dart. You are Dart the Digital Reindeer."

"Hmm, Dart. I like that a lot," he said prancing on his hooves a bit. "Thank you so much."

Sylvie smiled, "You're welcome. So, what else did you see?

"The most interesting thing I learned was about Santa Claus and all that he does. I would love to meet him and his reindeer."

Sylvie giggled, "I thought you'd be interested in that. We could email him and tell him we'd like to talk with him. But that might take some time, what with all the emails he must be getting this time of year."

"Well, that's no problem for me," Dart said. "I could move our email to the top of his list. Better still, he's online, and I can put us on his screen right now."

Sylvie sat forward in her chair. "You can do that?"

"Sure, nothing to it."

"How exciting, let's go."

"Santa was at the North Pole reviewing a list of e-presents,
when his monitor flickered and Dart and Sylvie appeared."

"Well, well," Santa chuckled, "What do we have here? I know you Sylvie, but who's your friend?"

"This is Dart the Digital Reindeer. I programmed him and by some magic he came to life in the virtual world."

"So nice to meet you, Dart. What can I do for you?"

"I wanted to meet you and your reindeer and see if there was anything I could do to assist you."

"Well, let's talk about that." Santa said, stroking his beard. "More than half of my toy orders and deliveries now go through the Internet. Let me bring in my elf in charge of online toys and

wishes and hear what she thinks. Vivian, can you come over here a minute?"

An elf appeared on the screen. "Sylvie, Dart, this is Vivian." Santa turned to the elf, "So, Vivian, Dart lives in the realm of computers and the Internet. Could you use some help with our online operations?"

Vivian blew a lock of hair from her face. "Are you kidding me? We're overwhelmed with cyber problems. Wait times for online help desks are a drag. I still can't resolve the order we placed two weeks ago for a remote-controlled airplane for Emma. Are these the kinds of things you could make easier, Dart?"

Dart nodded, "Let me take a look."

He disappeared for a few moments and then returned. "O boy, I can see all the difficulties you're having."

"By the way, I just fixed Emma's airplane order. It was hun up because of a typo. I corrected it and it will be delivered o time."

Vivian stared at Dart, astonished. "Wow, thanks so much."

"You're welcome."

Dart continued, "Where I live, there are thousands of
gressive programs and super computers running to make sure
t banks, stock brokers, and businesses make money from

Christmas. But there is precious little support when it comes collecting wishes from kids, getting their toys to them on time, helping with the true spirit of the season."

"That's very perceptive, Dart," Santa said.

"I'd love to work on that." Dart replied.

Vivian and Santa glanced at each other and nodded approvingly. Santa spoke in a deep voice, "Dart, I would like to make you one of my official reindeer. Would you agree to that?"

"I would be honored," Dart replied.

Santa asked, "Will you be my partner in the cyber world?"
His chest swelled, "I will."
Sylvie had tears in her eyes. "I'm so proud of you," she whispered.
"Actually, Dart, I've been waiting some time for you to come along," Santa said. "Welcome home."

Suddenly realizing something, Sylvie held up both hands to pause the conversation and said forcefully, "Wait a minute, I think I see what's going on here." She turned to Santa. "You knew that creating a digital reindeer depended on me having a powerful computer. Being Santa, you probably had a hand in getting me my Christmas present early — and in bringing Dart to life. Right?"

Santa winked and smiled, "Sylvie, you're a very bright girl."
Everyone paused to appreciate what Sylvie and Santa had just said. Finally, Santa broke the silence, "Now, we all have important things to do. Let's get going."

Santa and Vivian said goodbye, leaving Sylvie and Dart alone in her room. Lilly was asleep on the bed, dreaming of chasing a squirrel, her legs moving slightly.

Sylvie reached out to Dart, putting her hand on the screen.

"I love you, Dart." Sylvie said. "I hope you won't be too busy to visit me."

Dart raised his hoof and placed it next to Sylvie's hand.

"I love you too. We have a special bond. I will always have time for you," he promised.

They stood that way for a few moments, then Dart said, "I had best get to work now. See you later."

"Bye."

On Christmas morning, Emma, and countless other children from every corner of the world, were delighted to get the very thing they had wished for, thanks to Dart the Digital Reindeer.

Made in the USA
Coppell, TX
21 September 2021